BIRDS HAVE SEEDS.
BEES HAVE HONEY.
CAN A BEAR HAVE A GIRLFRIEND
BECAUSE HIS DADDY HAS MONEY?

Rich Ronald Grizzington III wants to date Bonnie Brown, but Bonnie isn't sure she likes the stuck-up cub. Brother Bear is sure, though—sure he *hates* any cub who wants to date Bonnie.

Can Bonnie's heart be won with fancy restaurants and expensive gifts?

Can Brother control his jealousy?

And why are Too-Tall and his gang trying to break into Ronald's school locker?

## BIG CHAPTER BOOKS

# The Berenstain Bears and the

# BIG DATE

## by the Berenstains

**A BIG CHAPTER BOOK™**

Random House New York

http://www.randomhouse.com/
http://www.berenstainbears.com/

*Library of Congress Cataloging-in-Publication Data*
Berenstain, Stan, 1923–
The Berenstain Bears and the big date / by the Berenstains.
    p.  cm. — (A big chapter book)
Summary: Brother Bear experiences jealousy when his friend Bonnie agrees
to go out on a date with the rich and spoiled Ronnie Grizzington III.
ISBN 0-679-88941-8 (trade). — ISBN 0-679-98941-2 (lib. bdg.)
[1. Jealousy—Fiction. 2. Wealth—Fiction. 3. Bears—Fiction. ]
I. Berenstain, Jan, 1923– .
II. Title. III. Series: Berenstain, Stan, 1923–  . Big chapter book.
PZ7.B4483Bebcf 1998
[Fic]—dc21
                                                        97-23457

Printed in the United States of America 10  9  8  7  6  5  4  3  2  1

BIG CHAPTER BOOKS is a trademark of Berenstain Enterprises, Inc.

# Contents

# Chapter 1
# A New Face

Another spring had come to Bear Country, and as cubs gathered in the schoolyard of Bear Country School to wait for the morning bell, there were signs that it wasn't just the birds and the bees who were thinking of romance. Bermuda McBear was flirting with Cool Carl King. Gil Grizzwold was flirting with Babs Bruno. And, of course, spring wouldn't have been spring without Queenie McBear flirting, too.

Queenie rarely flirted with just one cub. And today was no exception. At first she flirted a little with her on-again, off-again boyfriend, Too-Tall Grizzly. Then she pranced over to Barry Bruin, put her arm in his, and whispered something in his ear. Barry blushed. Suddenly he noticed Too-Tall glaring at him and went a bit pale. He pulled away from Queenie and ran over to a group of his friends.

"Hey, Barry, where ya goin'?" teased Queenie, hurrying after him.

"As far away from you as I can get," said Barry. "Your boyfriend's giving me the evil eye."

"Hey, Barry," said Brother Bear. "I hear Too-Tall wants to work out with you in the gym."

"Why?" said Barry.

"So he can turn you into his punching

bag," said Brother. Everyone laughed. Except Barry, that is.

"Come on, Barry," whined Queenie. "Play along for a little longer. At least until the big guy realizes I'm just trying to make him jealous."

But it looked as though Too-Tall had already come to that realization. Suddenly he gave Queenie a big grin, blew her a kiss, and turned back to his gang.

"Humph!" said Queenie. "That big lug's getting harder and harder to string along. What we need around here is a new face or two for me to flirt with—" Suddenly Queenie broke off. She was looking out toward the front gate. "Well, *hello*," she purred. "What have we here?"

A sleek black limousine had pulled up to the gate, and a uniformed chauffeur was opening the rear door. Out stepped a cub dressed in a suit and tie.

"Who's he?" asked Barry.

"Beats me," said Queenie.

"Why's he all dressed up?" asked Sister Bear.

Cousin Fred shrugged. "Maybe he's a substitute disciplinarian for Mr. Grizzmeyer."

"Or the poster boy for some new dress code Mr. G's about to announce," cracked Lizzy Bruin.

But it was Bonnie Brown who had a serious answer to Sister's question. "Judging from the chauffeured limousine," she said, "I'd guess the expensive suit and tie are just another way for that cub's parents to show everyone else how much money they have."

"Very logical, Bonnie," said Ferdy Factual. "You are, no doubt, correct."

"How'd you know that?" asked Sister.

"Don't forget," said Bonnie, "Squire and Lady Grizzly are my uncle and aunt. Every now and then they drop a hint that I should wear some fancy dress to school."

"Hmm," said Queenie, gazing dreamily at the new cub as he entered the schoolyard, elegant leather briefcase in hand. "I wonder if he has a girlfriend. If he does, he probably buys her lots of expensive gifts. And if he doesn't, it's about time he got one..."

"Really, Queenie," scoffed Ferdy. "Don't tell me you've decided to go after him just because he's rich!"

"And why shouldn't I?" said Queenie.

Ferdy folded his arms and gave a bored yawn. "Because money isn't important," he said.

"Oh, is that so?" said Queenie. "And what *is* important?"

"Brains," said Ferdy.

"That's just what bears say who don't have a lot of money," said Queenie.

"And *that*," said Ferdy, "is just what bears say who don't have a lot of brains!"

Queenie shot Ferdy a nasty look.

"*I* say go for it, Queenie," urged Barry. "Anything to get you off *my* back."

But Queenie didn't need any urging. She was already skipping off toward the new cub.

BRAINS.

## Chapter 2
## A Name for the Face

It had been hard not to notice the gleaming limousine at the front gate, and now practically every cub in the schoolyard was watching as Queenie spoke to the new cub. She frowned when he answered her. He spoke again, and she put her hands on her hips.

"I wonder what he said," said Sister.

"I don't know," said Lizzy. "But Queenie sure looks frustrated."

"Uh-oh," said Barry. "The new cub is about to meet our local gang leader."

Too-Tall stomped over to the new cub and glared down at him. But as soon as the cub spoke up, Too-Tall grinned and pointed over to Brother and Sister's group.

"He's coming over here," said Cousin Fred.

"Wonderful," said Ferdy sarcastically. "Try to look rich, everyone."

The new cub approached the group and looked from one girl cub to another. "Which of you is Bonnie Brown?" he said. He didn't say it as if he were asking for information. He said it as if he were *demanding* information—as if he had a right to know and the cubs had an obligation to tell him.

"That's me," said Bonnie.

The new cub smiled warmly at her. "Pleased to make your acquaintance," he said. "Let me introduce myself. I am Ronald Grizzington III. But you can call me Ronnie."

"Hi, Ronnie," said Brother, putting out his hand to shake.

The new cub looked down at Brother's hand as if it were covered with some icky fungus. "That's *Ronald* to you," he said coldly, then turned back to Bonnie with another warm smile. "My father, Ronald Grizzington II, is Squire Grizzly's new busi-

THAT'S <u>RONALD</u> TO YOU.

ness partner. They've joined forces to build a new multiplex movie theater across from Bear Country Mall. My father has built them all over Bear Country, you know. You might have seen him recently on that television show 'Lifestyles of the Rich and Well-Known.' Anyway, it's very nice to meet you." He glanced around at the others. "And your groupies, too, I suppose. See you later, Bonnie." He walked off to stand all alone by the fence.

"Groupies?" said Sister. "What do you suppose he meant by that?"

Bonnie sighed. "I hate to admit it," she said, "but he thinks you're all just hanging around me because my aunt and uncle are rich."

"*What?*" cried Brother. "That snob!"

"He's obviously a cub with a very shallow personality," sniffed Ferdy.

"Shallow personality, *deep pockets*," said Queenie, who had just rejoined the group.

"*Empty* deep pockets where *you're* concerned," Barry teased.

"Okay, I admit it," said Queenie. "I did my best, but he just kept asking where Bonnie was. Guess I don't stand a chance with him."

"Don't give up hope," said Bonnie. "He only wanted to meet me because his father is my uncle's new business partner."

"Don't be so sure," said Queenie. "You're the only cub he's shown the slightest interest in since he got here. Maybe he wants to date you."

The bell rang, and the cubs headed for the front door. *I sure hope not,* thought Bonnie as she followed her friends into school. *Because I don't think I like Ronald Grizzington III.*

## Chapter 3
## Dinner and a Movie

That afternoon the cubs were walking home from school, talking about the events of the day. Brother bragged about knocking Too-Tall out of a dodge ball game at recess. Sister had beaten Lizzy at hopscotch. Cousin Fred had gotten a perfect score on a science quiz. Only Bonnie had nothing to tell. She stared down at the pavement in front of her as she walked, lost in thought.

"A penny for your thoughts, Bonnie," said Brother.

She looked up. "Huh? Oh, nothing."

Sister snickered. "She's thinking about Ronald 'You-Can-Call-Me-Ronnie' Grizzington III. He talked to her again in the hall after lunch. I saw them. Do I get the penny?"

"You get zip," said Brother, obviously annoyed at the mere mention of the new cub. "What did he want, Bonnie?"

"Oh, nothing," said Bonnie. "Just said he'd see me tomorrow."

But when she got to Grizzly Mansion, Bonnie told a very different story to Squire and Lady Grizzly. They were in the drawing room, having afternoon tea.

"I heard that you met young Ronnie Grizzington today," said Lady Grizzly when Bonnie walked in. "His mother just phoned me."

Bonnie nodded.

"And?" said Squire Grizzly.

For a long moment Bonnie didn't answer. She seemed lost in thought again. Finally she said, "He asked me out on a date Friday night. He wants to take me to dinner and a movie."

"Oh, how nice!" said Lady Grizzly.

"Excellent!" cried Squire Grizzly. "Which fine restaurant is he taking you to? The Red

Berry? The Silver Salmon? The Land of Trout and Honey?"

Bonnie looked puzzled. "I assumed he meant the Burger Bear—"

"Nonsense!" said the squire. "I'm sure Ronnie has something better in mind than the Burger Bear."

"Your uncle's quite right, dear," said Lady Grizzly. "You must phone Ronnie right away and find out where he's taking you. So you'll know exactly what to wear."

"But I haven't accepted yet," Bonnie mumbled.

For a moment the room was so silent that a dropped pin would have made a noise like a cannon firing.

"Why not?" asked Squire Grizzly.

"For one thing, I'm not sure I like him," said Bonnie.

"What's not to like?" said the squire.

"He's rich. And his father is my new business partner: Ronald Grizzington II, the Multiplex King!"

"Oh, that has such a nice ring to it, dear," said Lady Grizzly. "Does that make young Ronnie the Multiplex Prince?"

"You betcha," said the squire. "*Crown* Prince!"

"But there's another thing," said Bonnie. "I'm worried about how Brother will take it if I accept."

Lady Grizzly frowned. "Why on earth are you worried about Brother Bear?" she asked. "After all, you're not going steady with him. I realize that whenever you go to the Burger Bear or the movies, it's always with Brother. But those aren't really *dates*. You're just best friends. Isn't that right, dear?"

"Well...I guess so," said Bonnie.

"Now, I really must tell you something, dear," said Lady Grizzly. "You know how fond your uncle and I are of Brother Bear—and of the whole Bear family, for that matter. But you'll have to admit that they aren't exactly...how shall I put it?...*at our level of society*. Brother isn't really the perfect match for you, dear. Your uncle and I feel that young Ronnie Grizzington is...how shall I say it?...*more your type*."

*He's rich and stuck-up*, thought Bonnie.

*That makes him my type?* But all she said was "I have to think it over, Auntie. I'm going to my room now."

As she left the drawing room, Bonnie heard her aunt call after her, "Besides, dear, since Mr. Grizzington *is* your uncle's new partner, it would be rather *rude* to refuse…"

## Chapter 4
## Queenie's Advice

By dinnertime at Grizzly Mansion, Bonnie still hadn't decided what to do about the date. While Squire and Lady Grizzly devoured their grilled brook trout, Bonnie just picked at hers. And when Greeves the butler served fresh blackberries for dessert, Bonnie ate only a few before excusing herself and going back upstairs to her room.

It was quite a predicament. She'd always known that her aunt and uncle were kind of stuck-up about being rich, but she loved them both very much and didn't want to disappoint them. On the other hand, there was Ronald "You-Can-Call-Me-Ronnie" Grizzington III. Stuck-up grownups who were your aunt or uncle was one thing. But a stuck-up cub who was a perfect stranger was another! And what about poor Brother? Of course, Bonnie knew they weren't going steady. But she wasn't always sure that Brother knew it…

The phone ringing snapped Bonnie out of her reverie. It was Queenie. She wanted to know if the math homework Teacher Bob had assigned was due the next day or the day after.

"Day after," said Bonnie.

"Great!" said Queenie. "That means I can

go to the Burger Bear tonight. You know what they say: Never do today what you can put off till tomorrow."

"Yeah, I guess," said Bonnie glumly.

"Hey, you sound kind of down, girl," said Queenie. "What's wrong?"

Bonnie told her about the big date proposal.

"Well, aren't *you* the lucky one!" said Queenie.

"I'm not so sure about that," said Bonnie. "My aunt and uncle think I should go out with Ronnie just because he's rich and his father is Uncle's new business partner. They call Ronnie the Multiplex Prince—like he's some kind of royalty."

"So what?" said Queenie. "Who cares what they think? What's important is what *Ronnie* thinks. And I bet he thinks you're cute and smart and interesting."

"You really think so?" said Bonnie.

"Sure," said Queenie. "All the other boys think you're cute and smart and interesting. Why shouldn't Ronnie?"

"Hmm," said Bonnie. "Maybe you're right. But he's so stuck-up!"

"Give the poor cub a break!" said Queenie. "He just moved to town and he doesn't

know anybody yet. He'll loosen up in a day or two."

"Why are you playing Cupid, Queenie?" asked Bonnie. "I thought you'd be...well, you know..."

"Jealous?" said Queenie. "Gimme a break! You know me, Bonnie. I was jealous for about five minutes, then I got over it."

Bonnie laughed. It was true. No cub in Bear Country School got over disappointments faster than Queenie.

"But there's another thing that bothers me about this date," said Bonnie.

"Let me guess," said Queenie. "You're

worried about Brother. That's silly, Bonnie. You and Brother aren't going steady. And neither are you and Ronnie, for heaven's sake! It's just a date. One measly little date! Besides, there might be a nice gift in it for you."

"That's not important," said Bonnie.

"Who said it was important?" said Queenie. "I just said it was nice!"

Bonnie laughed again.

"I think you should call Ronnie right this minute and tell him you'll go out with him," said Queenie. "Let me break it to Brother tomorrow morning at school. I'll let you know what he says. But I'm telling you, there's nothing to worry about."

If Bonnie had had more sense, she might have thought back to the last time she'd taken Queenie's advice. She would have had to give up thinking after a while, because the truth of the matter was that she had *never* taken Queenie's advice about anything. There was a good reason for that: Queenie's advice was famous for being *bad* advice. But at that point Bonnie wasn't thinking sensibly. She was looking for a reason—any reason at all—not to disappoint her aunt and uncle.

So she took the personal card Ronnie Grizzington had given her from her backpack, picked up the phone, and punched in the number on the card. "Hello, Mrs. Grizzington?" she said. "This is Bonnie Brown. Is Ronnie there?"

## Chapter 5
# Well, Are You Jealous?

The next morning, Brother arrived at the schoolyard before Bonnie. And Queenie was waiting for him. She ran up to him the moment he was inside the gate. "Guess what?" she said. "Bonnie's going out on a date with Ronnie Grizzington, *the Multiplex Prince!* Saturday night!"

Brother just stared blankly at her.

"I'm only telling you because you're *not* her boyfriend," said Queenie. "Otherwise, I'd never have the nerve. Ronnie really likes Bonnie, and she likes him, too. Ronnie and Bonnie—sounds kinda catchy, doesn't it? I'll bet he takes her to an expensive restaurant.

*And* buys her a really expensive gift. Well, are you jealous?"

Somehow Brother managed to twist his blank stare into a casual smile. Queenie was obviously trying to get a jealous reaction from him so she'd have some juicy gossip to spread around school that day. Sure, he was jealous. With a capital J. But he wasn't going to let *her* know.

"Why should I be jealous?" Brother said mildly. "Bonnie and I are best friends, not girlfriend and boyfriend. I think it's great that she's going out on a date with someone else—er, uh, not that what *we* go out on are *dates*…"

"Then what are they?" asked Queenie.

"Well," said Brother, "they're…sort of…er, uh…*activities*."

Queenie smiled slyly. "Oh, *activities*," she said. "Well, then, aren't you jealous that

OH, ACTIVITIES.

someone else is horning in on your *activities?*"

Brother looked Queenie right in the eye and said, "Of course not. And you can tell all your friends I said so. Your enemies, too."

As Queenie skipped off to hang out with her friends, Brother could feel bursts of jealousy going off like fireworks inside him. It wasn't a good feeling. It was a terrible feeling, like the feeling you get when you come down with the flu—only worse. It had been a long time since he'd had that awful feeling. In fact, he'd had it only once before, when he thought Bonnie was planning to go to a school dance with Too-Tall. Luckily, that had turned out to be nothing but a false rumor.

*Wait a minute!* thought Brother. *Maybe this is just a false rumor, too!* Queenie was always starting rumors so she could spread them around and make herself look important. And whenever she was having trouble making Too-Tall jealous, she would try to make someone else's boyfriend jealous. Not that Brother was Bonnie's boyfriend, of course...

Brother felt better already. All he had to do now was ask Bonnie about the rumor, just to make doubly sure it wasn't true. But he wouldn't actually *ask* her about it, since then she'd think that he thought it *might* be true…

There was Bonnie now, getting out of the chauffeured limousine that Squire and Lady Grizzly had suddenly insisted she ride to school every morning. So as not to seem too eager, Brother hung around a group of friends for a few minutes, pretending to listen to Ferdy Factual lecture about his new science report entitled "Antimatter: Does It

Matter?" Then he strolled casually over to where Bonnie was talking to Queenie.

"Oops, gotta go," said Queenie. "See you guys later." She skipped off.

"Queenie's been spreading a silly rumor that you're going out on a date with Ronnie Grizzington," Brother told Bonnie. "Thought I ought to tell you right away, so you can nip it in the bud." He forced a chuckle. "You know that Queenie. They don't call her the Rumor Queen for nothing. Heh, heh."

Brother didn't like the way Bonnie was

looking at him. As if she was afraid to tell him something. "What's wrong?" he said. "It *is* just a silly rumor, isn't it?"

Bonnie sighed. "Queenie may still be the Rumor Queen," she said. "But this time it's not just a rumor."

Brother felt as if his insides were turning inside out. *Oh, no!* he thought. It wasn't a budding rumor. It was a budding *romance!*

On the outside, though, he managed to stay cool and calm. "No kidding?" he said. "Well, sometimes Queenie's right just by accident, I guess." He shuffled his feet, wondering what to say next. He had to be careful not to sound jealous. But he wanted so badly to know all the ugly details of the upcoming date. "Where is he taking you?" he asked.

"To dinner and a movie," Bonnie replied.

"Oh, really?" said Brother. "I'm surprised

the *Multiplex Prince* would stoop to watch a movie in our little old-fashioned movie theater." *Oops*, he thought. *There I go again.*

Bonnie's eyes showed suspicion. "You aren't jealous, are you?" she asked.

Brother pretended to be shocked. "*Me? Jealous?* Come on, Bonnie. You know me better than that. It's just that I don't like him very much."

Bonnie looked away. "I know what you mean," she murmured. "But he'll loosen up in a day or two…"

Brother was steaming as he rejoined Ferdy's group. And, as it turned out, so was Ferdy's group.

"Did you see what that new cub just did to Harry McGill?" asked Cousin Fred.

"No," said Brother. "What happened?"

"His chauffeur parked in Harry's special wheelchair space at the front gate," said Fred. "Harry's mom pulled the van up behind them and honked, but they wouldn't move until Ronnie finished talking on his cell phone and got out. Can you believe the nerve of that cub?"

Brother shook his head. How could a single cub make such a jerk of himself in such a short time? And how could a nice cub like Bonnie go out on a date with him?

## Chapter 6
## An Afternoon Stroll

All day at school, Brother's friends were amazed at how well he seemed to be taking the news about Bonnie's date with the Multiplex Prince. But "seemed," not "well," was the word that really mattered. Beneath his outward calm, Brother's feelings were so twisted that if they'd had shapes, they would have looked like pretzels.

He wasn't just feeling sorry for himself. He was angry, too. Angry at Bonnie, naturally. But *especially* angry at Ronald Grizzington III. At least once a minute he would replay in his mind the scene of his first meeting with the new cub. It was like watching a scene from a bad movie over and over. Brother would put out his hand and say, "Hi, Ronnie." And then the camera would zoom in on Ronnie's haughty expression as he looked down at Brother's hand and said, "That's *Ronald* to you." Then the camera would pull back to take in both the nasty little smile on Ronnie's face and the embarrassed look on Brother's. Every time he saw it in his mind, the scene made him queasy. But he couldn't seem to keep himself from playing it over and over and over…

That afternoon, Brother didn't walk home

from school with his usual group of friends. He told them he needed to buy something at Biff Bruin's Pharmacy, and set off toward town. He did, in fact, go downtown, but he didn't stop at Biff Bruin's. He walked right past and kept going. Past the computer store, past the Red Berry restaurant, past Town Hall and the town square, and off toward the outskirts of town. He didn't really know where his feet were carrying him, but it was obvious that they were taking him in the opposite direction from home.

All the while, he played new scenes in his head: scenes of things that hadn't happened—but which very well *might* happen. In one, Bonnie beamed at Ronnie as he handed her a beautifully wrapped gift. Then she opened it and let out a squeal of delight. In another, Bonnie and Ronnie were sitting together in a darkened movie theater, watching a romantic movie. Ronnie had his arm across the back of Bonnie's seat, so that they were snuggled up close together. Before Brother could stop the scene, Ronnie leaned even closer to Bonnie and *kissed* her on the cheek…

Those scenes led to others: scenes of things that hadn't happened and *wouldn't* happen. In one, Ronnie fell and scraped his shin as he stepped onto the front porch of Grizzly Mansion for his date with Bonnie. In another, Ronnie opened his wallet to pay for dinner at the Red Berry, only to find it empty, while Bonnie looked on in shame and embarrassment.

As he walked, Brother realized that these last scenes were pictures of his own wishes. He felt ashamed of himself. He had always thought of himself as a nice cub, a good

cub, a cub who was kind to others and wished them no harm. And so did Mama and Papa, Gramps and Gran, Sister and Cousin Fred, and all his friends. How could he tell any of them about his jealous thoughts and feelings? He couldn't. That must be why he was walking away from home, away from his own neighborhood and the neighborhoods of his friends and relatives. But where was he going?

He was now far enough from town that it looked small in the distance when he glanced over his shoulder. He was on the highway out of town, and Birder's Woods loomed ahead. Pretty soon he reached Parts R Us, Two-Ton Grizzly's auto parts lot. He walked along the fence, past the rear gate, and through the scruffy woods in back until he entered a small clearing.

And there, at last, he stopped. Right on the doorstep of the Too-Tall gang's clubhouse.

## Chapter 7
# Talkin' Business

*Why?* thought Brother. *Why am I here?* He felt an urge to knock on the clubhouse door. But what would he say to the gang?

Suddenly the door opened and Vinnie peered out. He looked very surprised. Over his shoulder he said, "I was right, boss, someone's here. Come see who it is."

Too-Tall appeared in the doorway. A big smile spread across his face. "Well, hello there, Brother Bear," he said. "I had a funny feeling we might be seein' you this afternoon. Come on in."

As Brother stepped inside, Vinnie said, "Whaddya mean, boss? Why would Brother come here this afternoon? He *never* comes here."

"That's 'cause he's never had a problem quite like the one he's got now," said Too-Tall.

Skuzz and Smirk chuckled. But Vinnie still didn't understand. He stared at Brother and said, "So what're ya doin' here?"

Brother shook his head. "I...I'm not really sure..."

Too-Tall laughed. "*I* know why you're here, Mr. Straight Arrow. You need some help. *Not* the kind of help you can get from your wimpy straight-arrow family and friends."

Vinnie looked from Too-Tall to Brother and back. "You mean he wants us to steal somethin' for him?"

"Shut up, knucklehead!" snapped Too-Tall. "Me and Brother are talkin' business."

He turned to Brother. "We'd be glad to help you in your time of need, Mr. Goody Two Shoes. In fact, we'll do it for free. I been watchin' that new cub, and I don't like him one bit. We'll take care of him for you. That's what you came here for, ain't it?"

When Brother didn't answer, Too-Tall said, "Oh, I get it. You're too much of a goody two shoes wimp to say yes. I got a system for helpin' guys like you. If you *don't* want our help, say so right now. If you *do* want it, don't say anything."

But Brother didn't hear Too-Tall—not after he said, "That's what you came here for, ain't it?" Because he was lost in thought. It was amazing the way Too-Tall had read his mind—even before he *himself* had understood! He thought about the scenes of bad things happening to Ronnie Grizzington. While he'd been playing those scenes in his mind, his feet had carried him straight to Too-Tall's clubhouse. Hardly a coincidence!

*Oh, no!* thought Brother. *I can't have Too-Tall do anything to Ronnie Grizzington! At least, not on my account!*

Without saying another word, Brother turned on his heels and ran out of the club-house.

"Well, boss," said Smirk, with one of his famous smirks, "I guess we've got our answer."

Skuzz laughed. "Boy, what a goody-goody wimp!"

But Vinnie still looked puzzled. "I don't get it, boss," he whined. "Who are we supposed to take care of?"

## Chapter 8
## A Prank Fit for a Prince

After explaining the situation to dimwitted Vinnie, Too-Tall asked the gang for ideas on how they could "take care of" Ronald Grizzington III.

"That's a no-brainer, boss," said Smirk. "We'll just threaten to beat him up if he goes through with the big date."

"*You're* a no-brainer," said Too-Tall.

"What good would it do to threaten a cub whose rich daddy can hire a bunch of bodyguards to protect him?"

"Sorry, boss," said Smirk. "I didn't think of that."

"That's it, boss!" cried Vinnie. "The whole problem with this cub is that he's rich. If we steal all the Grizzingtons' money, Ronnie won't be able to go on his big date 'cause he'll be broke!"

Too-Tall just stared at Vinnie for a moment. Then, in the most sarcastic tone of voice he could muster, he said, "Good idea, Vinnie. Why don't you go over in the corner by yourself and work out all the details. Meanwhile, the rest of us'll try to come up with a *sensible* idea!"

His feelings hurt, Vinnie moped while the others thought. After a while Skuzz said, "I got it, boss! I hear Ronnie's been braggin' about how he's gonna buy some diamond earrings to give Bonnie when he picks her up for their big date. We could 'borrow' the earrings just long enough to booby-trap the box with a paint bomb. When Bonnie opens it, *bingo!* She'll never forgive him!"

"Not bad, Skuzz-brain," said Too-Tall.

"But what if he has the box gift-wrapped

at the jewelry store?" asked Smirk. "How could we booby-trap it?"

Too-Tall shook his head. "Nah," he said. "If I know that stuck-up little cub as well as I think I do, he's not gonna have the earrings gift-wrapped at the store. He'll bring 'em to school so he can show 'em off to everybody first, then have his fancy butler gift-wrap 'em. When he leaves his briefcase in his locker at lunchtime, we'll 'borrow' the earrings for a few minutes. Remember, guys: the locker *I* can't get into doesn't exist!"

"That's right, boss!" Vinnie piped up, eager to get back into Too-Tall's good graces. "And if it doesn't exist, who cares if you can't get into it?"

Too-Tall just stared at Vinnie again. "Good thinkin', pal," he said. "I don't know what we'd do without ya."

## Chapter 9
# A Misunderstanding?

Sure enough, just as Too-Tall had predicted, Ronald Grizzington III stood in the middle of the schoolyard the next morning, showing off a pair of diamond earrings to anyone who wanted to see. (And to more than a few cubs who *didn't* want to see, too.) When Bonnie's limo arrived, he quickly closed the box and slipped it into his briefcase. Too-Tall and the gang exchanged winks. Their plan was on track.

Later, the gang's lunchtime locker caper went off without a hitch. As Too-Tall had said, the locker he couldn't get into didn't exist. And Ronnie Grizzington's locker certainly existed. It was hard to miss. He had

advertised its existence by putting large gold stickers spelling out *Ronald Grizzington III* on the door. Too-Tall's nimble fingers found the combination of the lock in an instant. It was left to Skuzz, the gang's booby trap expert, to finish the job.

By afternoon recess, everything was ready for the big date. The day before, Lady Grizzly had taken Bonnie shopping at Bloomingbear's for a new dress to wear. Now Ronnie had his diamond earrings and Too-Tall had booby-trapped them for Brother. All that was left was for Too-Tall to decide

whether or not to let Brother in on their little secret. He talked it over with the gang. Skuzz and Smirk voted for telling Brother what they'd done. But Vinnie was doubtful. "I don't know, boss," he said. "If you tell him, it's gotta be under one condition: that he be sworn to *absolute secrecy*."

"Secrecy?" laughed Too-Tall. "You gotta be kiddin', birdbrain! Brother's not gonna rat on us. He's the one who told us to do it in the first place!" And, with that, he strolled over to Brother, who looked for all the world like a lost soul.

"Hey, there, Brother Bear," said Too-Tall. "I've got some info that just might lift your spirits a little."

Brother glanced up at Too-Tall with eyes that looked as if they hadn't seen the backs of his eyelids all night. "Lift my spirits?" he said. "It'd probably be easier to lift an elephant."

Too-Tall leaned down and whispered in Brother's ear. "You know those diamond earrings the Multiplex Prince was showin' off this morning?" Brother nodded. "You might wanna hide in the bushes at Grizzly Mansion and watch when Ol' Ronnie Boy gives them to You-Know-Who. Pay special attention when You-Know-Who *opens the box...*"

Brother frowned. "Why?" he said. "What are you talking about?"

Too-Tall smiled. "Oh, you wanna play dumb about it? Okay, that's cool. Anyway, we did what you wanted."

"What *I* wanted?" said Brother. "But I never told you to do anything."

"Of course you didn't," said Too-Tall, with a chuckle. He winked at Brother and elbowed him in the ribs. "And what you didn't tell us to do, we went and did for you. We fixed Ronnie 'That's-*Ronald*-to-You' Grizzington III. And *good*. We booby-trapped those fancy earrings with a red paint bomb. When your once-and-future girlfriend opens that box—boy, is *she* gonna be red-faced!"

Brother's eyes widened. "Oh, no!" he cried. "You *didn't!*"

Too-Tall laughed. "Why ya puttin' on such a show? Nobody's listenin' to us."

"There's been a misunderstanding!" said Brother.

"There sure has," Too-Tall chuckled. "It happened when Rich Boy and You-Know-Who thought they could treat you this way. *You,* a cub with powerful friends like Yours Truly!"

"You've got to call it off, big guy!" said Brother.

It suddenly dawned on Too-Tall that

Brother wasn't play-acting. "Call it off?" he said, frowning. "Too late for that, my friend. The deed's been done. Boy, you're an even bigger wimp than I thought."

Brother's stomach did flips as he watched Too-Tall strut back to his gang. Bonnie's big date would be ruined, and it would be *his* fault! And not just her date—her beautiful new dress, too! He had to tell her. At least, he *ought* to tell her...

But no sooner had Brother realized what he ought to do than a new scene began playing in his mind. In it, Bonnie tore the wrapping paper off Ronnie's gift and opened the box. The camera zoomed in on

her face as red paint splattered it, then pulled back to show both Ronnie's shocked expression and Bonnie's furious one... Brother couldn't help snickering. That scene made him feel good all over.

*Oh, no*, thought Brother. *I know what I* should *do... but what* will *I do...?*

That afternoon, Brother didn't go straight home from school. Instead, he headed into the woods behind school and made a bee-line for his Thinking Place.

## Chapter 10
## To Tell or Not to Tell...

To tell or not to tell...

...that was the question. Brother sat on his favorite rock at the Thinking Place and pondered his dilemma. It was a peaceful spot, with birds twittering and squirrels darting to and fro in the trees. But there was no peace in Brother's heart. He was torn between telling Bonnie about the paint bomb and watching her and Ronnie get what they deserved.

But did they *really* deserve it? Brother's thinking went back and forth. One moment, his brain told him they didn't deserve it; the

next moment, his jealous heart told him they did. One moment, his brain formed a perfectly clear image of the right thing to do; the next moment, that image disappeared in a fog of jealousy.

Thinking clearly about what to do wasn't easy. He was so confused about his jealous thoughts and feelings. He was ashamed of them, too. But, at the same time, they were so *powerful*...

Suddenly Brother remembered a conversation he had had with Mama. At the time, he hadn't really taken it to heart, because Mama was talking about Too-Tall's jealous behavior toward Queenie McBear, and that was *Too-Tall's* problem, not his. But now he realized that what Mama had said applied to him, too. He remembered in particular one thing she'd said: "Jealousy is nothing to get too worried about."

Brother felt less ashamed when he remembered that conversation. But there was something else he recalled. Mama had said, "You shouldn't worry too much about feeling jealous. But what you *should* worry about is letting jealous thoughts and feelings persuade you to *do* bad things."

Mama had a real knack for putting things in ways that made sense. And this time was no exception. Brother realized that he was on the verge of letting his jealous thoughts

and feelings persuade him to do a bad thing: *not* tell Bonnie about the paint bomb. He jumped up. He would go straight home and phone Bonnie…

With a groan, Brother sat back down on the rock and put his head in his hands. If only it were that simple! But there was another part of the dilemma. A part that didn't seem to have anything to do with knowing the difference between right and wrong. If he didn't tell Bonnie about the paint bomb, she might never find out how it got there. Ronnie Grizzington III had already made a bunch of enemies. There were a lot of cubs who might play a prank on him: Too-Tall, Cool Carl King, Queenie, Harry McGill, even Ferdy Factual. But if he *did* tell Bonnie, she would know that *he* was behind the prank! She'd never believe the truth: that it was all due to a misunderstanding between Too-Tall and him. That would sound like a story he'd made up to get himself off the hook. If he told, Bonnie would never forgive him for going to Too-Tall for help. And neither would anyone else! He'd lose all his friends! And what would his family think of him?

It was quite a while before Brother remembered to glance at his watch. Dinnertime already! The big date was just a couple of hours away. He still didn't have a clue about what he was going to do. And, on top of everything, his backside was numb from sitting on that darn rock!

Stiffly, Brother got up and trudged homeward.

## Chapter 11
## SPLAT!

Brother hardly ate any dinner that evening. Afterward, he went straight to his and Sister's room and sat on his bunk bed. He eyed the telephone on the night table. He reached for it, then pulled his hand back. He took a deep breath and reached for it again. Again he pulled his hand back. An image formed in his mind's eye, an image of Bonnie with red paint all over her face, yelling "I'll never speak to you again!" at Ronnie Grizzington. He grinned.

Brother hurried downstairs, where Papa sat in his easy chair reading the latest issue of *Fields and Streams* and Mama sat on the sofa reading the latest issue of *Tree House Beautiful*. "I'm going to the Burger Bear," he announced.

"All right, son," said Mama. "But don't stay out too late."

Brother took the front steps at a leisurely pace and headed downtown. But the moment he was out of sight of the tree house, he circled back toward Grizzly Mansion and picked up speed. *What am I doing?* he thought. *I should be calling Bonnie and warning her!* Then he pictured Bonnie yelling "I'll never speak to you again!" at Ronnie Grizzington and walked even faster.

Within minutes, Brother reached Grizzly Mansion. As usual, the front gate was closed and a guard was in the guardhouse. Brother found a spot out of sight of the guardhouse and climbed the fence. Safely inside, he scurried across the lawn and hid in some bushes near the front porch.

It wasn't long before the Grizzington limousine appeared at the front gate. The gate swung open, and the chauffeur drove the limo up the long drive and parked. Ronnie Grizzington waited for the chauffeur to come around and open the rear door for him. Every time Brother had seen him,

Ronnie had been wearing a different suit and tie. Tonight was no exception. In his hand was a small gift-wrapped box.

Ronnie went to the porch and rang the doorbell. Greeves the butler answered.

"Good evening, Master Ronald," he said. "I'll inform Bonnie that you've arrived. Oh, here she is now."

Bonnie appeared in her beautiful new dress and stood on the porch with Ronnie. She didn't look particularly happy or excited. In fact, she looked a bit glum. Ronnie handed her the gift and said, "I bought you a little something."

"Oh, you shouldn't have," said Bonnie, looking down at the gift in her hand.

"A girl like you deserves expensive gifts," said Ronnie. "Go ahead, open it."

Bonnie slowly removed the wrapping paper, which Ronnie took from her and crumpled into a ball. She placed her hand on the lid of the box.

Cowering in the bushes, Brother held his breath. *Oh, boy!* he thought. *Here it comes!* But at that instant he heard something

unexpected. It was almost like a little voice inside his head telling him to do the right thing. He knew what it was. It was his conscience.

Before Bonnie could lift the lid of the box, Brother leapt from the bushes. "Don't!" he cried. "Don't open it, Bonnie!"

Wide-eyed and open-mouthed, Bonnie and Ronnie stared at Brother. An angry frown came to Bonnie's face. "What in the world are *you* doing here?" she said.

Brother gave a sheepish grin. He felt his ears start to burn. He knew that meant he was blushing like crazy.

"He's obviously spying on us," said Ronnie. "And it's also obvious that he doesn't want you to open the box because he's jealous. *He* can't *afford* to buy you nice gifts like this!"

Bonnie glared at both of them. For a moment she wasn't sure which she disliked more: Brother's spying or Ronnie's snobbishness. But it didn't take her long to decide. *The nerve of that Brother Bear!*

She lifted the lid of the box.

SPLAT!

It was hard to tell who looked more

shocked: Bonnie or Ronnie. But Bonnie was certainly more red-faced.

"I…I tried, Bonnie," Brother said weakly. "I tried to warn you…"

The shock quickly faded from Bonnie's expression, and fury took its place, made all the more vivid by the bright red paint all over her face. She pointed a finger straight at Brother. "You didn't tell me not to open that box because you were jealous!" she cried. "You knew it was booby-trapped! Because *you booby-trapped it!*"

Brother was at a complete loss for words. He knew that Bonnie would never believe the truth. So he just turned and ran. He ran down the long drive to the front gate and headed for home.

## Chapter 12
## The Big Date

Back in his room, Brother lay on his bed with his head in his hands. In the war between his good side and his bad side, there had been no winner. He had chickened out when his bad side drew him to the gang's clubhouse and Too-Tall had offered to help. But when his good side had tried to warn Bonnie about the paint bomb, she had gotten splattered anyway. It seemed as if he couldn't do anything right—good *or* bad. And now he was sure to lose all his friends, too!

Meanwhile, Bonnie and Ronnie were in the back of the Grizzington limo, on their way to the Red Berry. Bonnie had changed from her paint-splattered dress into blue jeans and a jean jacket. It had embarrassed her to get such an expensive gift from Ronnie, and now she didn't want him to take her to an expensive restaurant, too. She had thought he would refuse to take her to the Red Berry because she was dressed in blue jeans. But as they rode into town, Ronnie said nothing. He seemed far away, as if his mind wasn't on the date at all.

Finally, Bonnie couldn't stand it any longer. "Let's not go to the Red Berry," she said. "I'd be embarrassed to go in dressed like this."

Ronnie looked at her clothes. "Oh, I see," he said. "I didn't notice what you were wearing. But where would we go?"

"I really feel like a cheeseburger," said Bonnie. "Let's go to the Burger Bear."

"Cheeseburger?" said Ronnie. "But don't you want something more than cheese in a bun for dinner?"

Bonnie stared at her date. "Ronald Grizzington III!" she said. "You've never *had* a cheeseburger, have you? You don't even know what it is!"

"To tell the truth," said Ronnie with a shrug, "I've never eaten in a restaurant that serves cheeseburgers." And then he said something that surprised Bonnie. "But if that's what you want, let's go to this Burger Bear place."

"You'll like it," said Bonnie, already feeling a little better about the date. "My uncle owns it, you know."

So they went to the Burger Bear. Ronnie took off his tie and suit jacket and left them in the limo. He ended up actually enjoying his first cheeseburger and fries. In fact, he

THAT'S <u>MISTER</u> BIG GUY TO YOU!

loosened up so much that he even said hi to Bonnie's friends who came by the booth. After a while, someone came by who wasn't a friend of Bonnie's. Not exactly an enemy, but not really a friend, either.

"Hi, big guy," said Bonnie. "What's up?"

"I didn't think I'd see the two of *you* around after your little mishap with that paint bomb," said Too-Tall.

Ronnie looked up, puzzled. "How did you know about that, big guy?"

"That's *Mister* Big Guy to you!" snarled Too-Tall. "Me and the gang were watchin' from behind the fence."

"You were?" said Bonnie. "Did Brother tell you he booby-trapped the gift?"

"Nah," said Too-Tall. " 'Cause *he* didn't booby-trap it. Me and the gang did. And *I* told *him* about it." Too-Tall went on to tell them all about the big misunderstanding.

"So Brother didn't really want you to plant the paint bomb?" said Bonnie when Too-Tall had finished.

"That's right," said Too-Tall. "And don't you forget it. That was one of the best paint-bomb pranks we've ever pulled. And I won't let some little wimp like Brother Bear steal the credit for it. So when you start spreadin' the story all over town, *get it right!"* And, with that, Too-Tall stalked back to the gang's booth.

Of course, Bonnie was overjoyed to hear that Brother hadn't planted the paint bomb. Now she felt sorry for him. For two reasons: one, because he'd felt so jealous that he'd thought about asking Too-Tall for help, and two, because she had falsely accused him of planting the paint bomb.

Too-Tall's news put a big damper on the big date. Bonnie hadn't really wanted to go through with it in the first place, and now all she wanted to do was talk to Brother and apologize for yelling at him. There was only one thing keeping her from calling off the rest of the date. She didn't want to hurt Ronnie's feelings, especially now that he was loosening up a little and not being so stuck-up.

By the time their limo reached the movie

theater, Bonnie couldn't stand it any longer. It couldn't be helped if Ronnie's feelings were hurt. She blurted out that she hadn't wanted to go on the date, that her aunt and uncle had pushed her into it because of the squire's business relationship with Ronnie's father.

Ronnie looked at her with amazement. He seemed stunned. For a moment Bonnie was afraid he might cry.

But he didn't. Not only did Ronnie not cry, he actually smiled. Then he threw his head back and laughed.

"What's so funny?" said Bonnie. "I thought you'd be upset."

"You don't understand!" cried Ronnie. "We're in the same boat!"

"Well," said Bonnie, "I can see that we're in the same *limo*, but—"

"No, really!" said Ronnie. "*I* only asked *you* out because my parents told me to! And they pushed me into it for exactly the same reason that your aunt and uncle pushed *you* into it!"

"But why didn't you say so earlier?" asked Bonnie.

"Because I didn't want to hurt your feelings!" said Ronnie.

Now it was Bonnie's turn to throw her head back and laugh. Ronnie joined in

again, and the two cubs laughed until they cried.

The window between the driver's seat and the passengers' compartment lowered. "Is everything all right, Master Ronald?" asked the chauffeur.

"Everything's fine, James," said Ronnie, wiping away tears.

"But aren't you going to the cinema?" asked James.

Ronnie looked up at the theater mar-
quee, which read: NOW SHOWING: FIELD
OF SCREAMS. "What's the movie?" he
asked Bonnie.

"It's a horror movie," she said. "I saw the
coming attractions last week. It's about dead
baseball players who come back as ghosts.
There's one scene where they chase a
farmer through a cornfield with baseball
bats."

Ronnie shuddered. "Sounds scary," he

said. "You know, I don't really like horror movies."

"Me neither," said Bonnie. "Why don't we just go home?"

Ronnie agreed and told James to head for Grizzly Mansion. On the way, he turned to Bonnie and said, "I really do like you, Bonnie. I hope we can still be friends."

"I think we can," said Bonnie. "But only if you're nicer to my other friends. Until tonight, you've acted pretty stuck-up toward them."

Ronnie apologized. He explained that his parents had always discouraged him from associating with what they called "ordinary" cubs. If he was seen being nice to "ordinary" cubs, he thought, his parents might hear about it and be disappointed.

"Well," said Bonnie, "if you ask me, it's time you started disappointing your parents a little. Just like I should disappoint my aunt and uncle once in a while."

"Ever since we left the Burger Bear," Ronnie admitted, "I've been thinking exactly the same thing. I know! My first act of independence will be to invite you and your friends to Grizzington Mansion for a croquet party!"

"Better make that a croquet *and volleyball* party," suggested Bonnie.

"Deal," said Ronnie.

And they shook hands on it.

## Chapter 13
# The Bear of Last Resort

As happy as Bonnie was to learn that Brother hadn't planted the paint bomb, Brother was even happier to get a phone call from Bonnie. And his joy knew no bounds when Bonnie said that Too-Tall had told her all about the big misunderstanding. She apologized for accusing him of planting the paint bomb.

"That's okay, Bonnie," said Brother. "You had a right to be angry. After all, I *was* spying on you."

"I'll admit spying was bad," said Bonnie. "But you *did* try to warn me at the last minute."

"I never should have gone to Too-Tall's

clubhouse with a big problem on my mind," said Brother. "If I hadn't, none of this would have happened."

"Well, at least it sounds like you learned your lesson," said Bonnie.

"You bet!" said Brother quickly. Then, a bit sheepishly, he added, "Just remind me what the lesson is."

"When you have a problem," said Bonnie, "Too-Tall is the *last* bear you should go to with it."

"Sort of the bear of last resort?" joked Brother.

"Actually, the bear of *no* resort!" said Bonnie. "By the way, Ronnie Grizzington is having a croquet and volleyball party at Grizzington Mansion on Sunday afternoon."

Brother's heart sank. *Uh-oh*, he thought. *Here we go again*. "Gee," he said softly. "That's great."

"Don't sound so depressed," said Bonnie. "You're invited, too! And so are all our friends!"

"No kidding?" cried Brother. "Awesome!"

# Chapter 14
## Party Payback

Grizzington Mansion was almost as big as Grizzly Mansion, and the front lawn had more than enough room for both a croquet

lawn and a volleyball court. Most of the invited cubs had never played croquet, and Ronnie patiently showed everyone the ins and outs of his favorite game. He was especially nice to Brother, who hadn't been sure how welcome he would be at Grizzington Mansion.

After croquet, they played volleyball and worked up quite a sweat. A maid brought out a tray filled with glasses of lemonade and served the cubs as they rested. A butler followed with another tray. On it was a gift-wrapped box. Ronnie took the box and handed it to Brother. "Just to show you there are no hard feelings," he said, "I bought you a new volleyball."

Brother didn't know what to say except, "Gee, thanks, Ronnie." He had been wanting a new volleyball for months, but had kept spending too much of his allowance on milk shakes at the Burger Bear.

"Go ahead," said Ronnie. "Open it."

Eagerly, Brother tore off the wrapping paper and lifted the lid off the cardboard box.

SPLAT!

The rest of the cubs fell down laughing as

Ronnie handed Brother a rag to wipe his paint-splattered face with.

"That," said Ronnie, "was for ruining the diamond earrings I bought with my hard-*un*earned money. If you'd warned us sooner, they could have been saved. Now we're even." He said it in a friendly, joking way, not a mean way. And then he grinned.

Brother couldn't help grinning, too. After all, it *was* funny. Together the two cubs burst into laughter. They laughed loud and long.

"Hey, Ronnie," said Barry Bruin. "Did you rig that paint bomb yourself?"

"Actually, no," said Ronnie. "Too-Tall's

friend—that Skuzz fellow—did it for me."

"How much did you have to pay him?" asked Cousin Fred.

"Nothing," said Ronnie. "Yesterday, I had James drive me out to Parts R Us. I walked around back to the gang's clubhouse and had a little talk with Too-Tall."

That raised quite a few eyebrows. "And you lived to tell the tale?" said Babs Bruno.

"Too-Tall was quite nice to me after I informed him I'd decided not to tell Chief Bruno about the paint bomb if he'd help me 'get' Brother," said Ronnie.

"That's still kind of surprising," said Queenie. "The big guy doesn't like to be pushed around."

"Oh, he made that quite clear," said Ronnie. "What saved me was that I went alone, without any bodyguards. He said it took a lot of courage. Actually, 'guts' is the word he used, I believe. He even shook my hand."

"Wow!" said Bonnie. "You've loosened up even more than I thought, Ronnie. But if you're already friends with Too-Tall, why didn't you invite him and the gang to the party? I'm sure they would have enjoyed watching Brother get splattered."

Ronnie looked over his shoulder at Grizzington Mansion, where Mr. and Mrs. Grizzington could be seen peeking out from behind the drapes of an upstairs room. "I thought it would be best not to push my parents too far too fast," he admitted. "It took some quick talking to persuade them to let me put up a volleyball net and invite all of *you*. But I assure you that Too-Tall and his gang will be on my party list next time."

Suddenly a deep voice bellowed, "In that case, we accept!" And out stepped Too-Tall

from behind a tree, with a big grin on his face. A moment later, Skuzz, Smirk, and Vinnie popped out from various bushes.

Ronnie looked at them in wonderment. "I'm glad to see you fellows," he said. "But how did you get past the guard?"

With a wink, Too-Tall answered, "Don't forget: the guard we can't get past doesn't exist!"

"Yeah, boss," said Vinnie. "And if he doesn't exist—"

"Chill out, birdbrain!" said Too-Tall. "It's a party, not a philosophy class!"

And the cubs all laughed as the maid hurried out with another tray of lemonade for the gang.

**Stan and Jan Berenstain** began writing and illustrating books for children in the early 1960s, when their two young sons were beginning to read. That marked the start of the best-selling Berenstain Bears series. Now, with more than one hundred books in print, videos, television shows, and even Berenstain Bears attractions at major amusement parks, it's hard to tell where the Bears end and the Berenstains begin!

Stan and Jan make their home in Bucks County, Pennsylvania, near their sons—Leo, a writer, and Michael, an illustrator—who are helping them with Big Chapter Books stories and pictures. They plan on writing and illustrating many more books for children, especially for their four grandchildren, who keep them well in touch with the kids of today.